A SINFUL PHONE CALL

(The Sin Club Book 2)

RACHELLE CHASE

ACKNOWLEDGMENTS

Special thanks—and all my love—to my family and my undying gratitude to my readers for continuing to read my books.

A WORD FROM THE AUTHOR

This is a work of fiction, not a guide to real life. As such, my characters don't use condoms.
But real people should in real life.

Follow the conversation at:
www.rachellechase.com/condom-conundrum-are-condoms-really-necessary-in-romance-novels/

1

"Hi, Shawn. I'm the woman who was wearing the short red dress, standing on the corner."

Damn.

Cringing at the words she'd just blurted, Sharice jabbed the pound key on the cell phone keypad to delete the voicemail message she'd just recorded. As the digital voice walked her through the instructions to rerecord her message, she stared out the windshield of her Lexus, idly noticing the after-eleven crowd in line in front of the new nightclub, Tantrum. Defying the chilly October air, the women wore their spaghetti-strap tops and tightest skirts, while standing proud in their three-inch strappy sandals.

She tried again.

"Hi, Shawn . . . This is Sharice. I met you outside of Tantrum last Friday. I was talking to my friend when you shouted your number out the window . . ."

My God. Are the pickings for a night of sex so slim that I have to resort to this? Just hang up.

"... and ..."

Hang up.

"... well ..."

Hang the fuck up.

But, damn, that man had been on her mind all week. It was once again Friday evening, and she somehow found herself cruising down the street in front of the club where they'd met. Her favorite song played on the radio—Kid Ink, crooning about how he was going to push her panties to the side—and got her all hot and bothered.

The same song had been playing softly from the depths of Shawn's Lex that night, too. Surely, that must be a sign. Just as the fact that his gleaming red car, identical to hers, was a sign. A sign that, unlike her last boyfriend, Darrell, and his 1990 Honda Civic, Shawn might actually treat her to dinner, instead of always crying broke. And Shawn's voice, as he'd practically begged her to call him, had sounded like liquid sex. That had been another sign.

The voice was a definite positive for a night of hot sex. For, if his technique was sad, she could just ask him to talk—and that sweet, slow, sexy tone would make up for any lack of finesse.

Sharice paused, about to delete her message again, when the song faded out on the radio and Tommy "Dr. Love" Jones came on.

"Now, that's a sinful song, isn't it?" He laughed. "It's definitely telling you to go out and sin, though not necessarily the way I'm advocating. I'm urging you, KPSX listeners, to go out and go for what you want, sin. Your happiness is just a sin away ..."

Dr. Love was right. It was about time she

"sinned." That is, do something she'd never done before. She turned her attention back to the phone.

". . . Call me at 510-555-1201," she finished.

Sharice clicked her phone off and tossed it onto the passenger seat, surprised to feel herself shaking from surplus adrenaline. How ridiculous that something as simple as calling a guy would spark the fight-or-flight response. On the other hand, maybe it wasn't so ridiculous, since she *never* called men first, period. She always waited for them to call her. Hell, she was no fool—she lived by the book *He's Just Not That Into You,* which was co-authored by Greg Behrendt.

Hence, she was committing a double sin—she was calling a guy first and she was calling a guy she hadn't even really met. And the only reason she'd broken her rule this time was because, well, it was kind of hard for a guy who didn't have her name or number to call her back.

So now what?

The line outside the club had grown another twelve feet since she'd arrived. Sharice did not do lines. Craning her neck forward, she looked to see if John was at the door. Yep. There he was, his bald, peanut-shaped head glistening in the soft light. He'd let her slide to the front of the line. There'd be no waiting tonight.

Sharice sighed. So what if she got in the club? Somewhere in between the time that she'd pulled out of her garage and pulled into this parking spot, Tantrum had lost its appeal. The effort it would take to make meaningless small talk with a dozen or more men, in hopes of meeting one she wanted to take home for the night seemed like too much effort. Kind of like finding her contact lens in the Pacific Ocean.

She'd been feeling like that a lot lately, which was why she'd been celibate for months. *Six* months, to be exact.

A group of loud-talking sistahs—whose long hair did a better job of covering their asses than their skirts did—sauntered past the car. Did they really think they looked good?

Stop being so bitchy.

She should just go home. Her attitude was not male-magnet material.

But she didn't want to go home. Friday night was a prime party night, for crying out loud. And it was time for her to get her game back on track.

Sharice pressed the pad of her finger against the screen, turning up the radio. The deep voice of Dr. Love filled the car.

". . . Good luck, man . . . You're on, Jessie. What's your sin?"

Jessie giggled.

Sharice rolled her eyes.

"Well, a couple of months ago, I did a striptease for my boyfriend. It was something I'd always wanted to do, but had never done before . . ."

Dr. Love made a sound of approval.

Sharice snorted. "That ain't nothing. I've done a hundred stripteases."

". . . only it wasn't my boyfriend who saw it. It was my neighbor."

"Damn. I haven't done *that,*" said Sharice.

Dr. Love laughed.

Jessie laughed. ". . . needless to say, the boyfriend's out and my neighbor is in."

"He's 'in'? Literally or figuratively?" asked Dr.

Love.

Jessie and Dr. Love shared a chuckle.

Sharice joined in.

"Let's just say he's the new man in my life. Our relationship is wonderful. He—"

Sharice snorted. "I was feeling you until you ruined things with a 'relationship.'" She pressed the screen again, cutting Jessie off in mid-sentence; Sharice shook her head. A person had a better chance of winning the lottery than ending up in a relationship that worked. What was up with most women who were desperate for the big R? Sharice had tried that, twice, believing that she'd found *the one* each time. Instead, she'd discovered Malcolm had been living on the down low, sleeping with men behind her back. And Darrell had been sleeping with anything in a skirt, including whichever of her so-called friends he could get into bed—Sharice's bed.

Nope. She was through with that. Fool me once, shame on you; fool me twice, shame on me. Well, she was not going to be anyone's fool anymore. So now she just looked for a brotha for a good time.

But, for some reason, the "good times" were feeling fewer and farther in between. And Sharice's attitude was getting more and more frustrated. Not to mention her libido. She shrugged, throwing off her depressing thoughts.

Well, she might as well go inside the club. As she reached for her keys, her cell phone rang.

She glanced at the display on her cell. It was Shawn. Sharice grinned, no longer nervous now that she was back on familiar ground—being pursued.

She pressed a button to connect the call. "I like a guy who goes after what he wants."

"Uh . . ."

Damn, she was good. The throaty voice worked every time.

"You *do* want something, don't you, Shawn?"

"Yeah . . . uh . . ."

She smiled. He was speechless, though the fact that he was surprised her a bit. From what little she'd been able to see of him in his car, the sly quirk of his lip—which passed for a smile—gave the impression that he was the type to have a snappy comeback.

"Well . . . ?" she prompted, converting the throatiness to a purr.

"Yes. Well. I'm not . . ."

He cleared his throat.

Sharice's smile widened.

"I'd like . . . you. Talk . . ."

She couldn't quite make out what he was saying, with the reception so bad. She'd only heard a few of the words and it sounded like he was far away, in a tunnel, with the wind blowing.

"What?"

". . . see you."

"You'd like to see me?" she repeated.

"Y . . ."

Was that a yes?

". . . now?" he asked.

"I can't hear you."

"Are you available now?"

She got it that time. He sounded like he was yelling, but his voice didn't register much louder. Where was he calling from?

Sharice paused. A woman should never appear too available, especially at 11:10 P.M. Even author Greg Behrendt would probably agree with that. She let her gaze drift back to Tantrum, to the line that now looped around the corner. There'd be a good-size crowd inside. Odds were, even she could find someone interesting inside.

But she had someone who might be interesting right here, right now.

Screw Greg Behrendt. She didn't care if Shawn wasn't "into" her because she had no intention of being "into" him. After all, she wasn't looking for a relationship. She didn't have to go by all the rules.

"What do you have in mind?" she asked.

2

"Fuck!" Jamal slammed his fist against the steering wheel of his 1986 Toyota Camry as the engine continued to churn futilely. He didn't know if he was cursing because the car wouldn't start—yet again—or because he'd just messed up. Not only had he stuttered and stammered like a prepubescent idiot, he'd asked this Sharice to meet him at a bar. A bar four miles away from the freeway shoulder where he and his car were now stuck.

Why the hell hadn't he just told her he wasn't Shawn—that she'd called the wrong number, like the five women before her?

Because of that damn sexy voice, that's why. Unlike the women before her, he wanted to know why a woman who sounded that good would call a number some dog had shouted during a drive-by. He'd never heard a voice like Sharice's this side of 1-900-FANTASY. He grimaced at the memory, still unable to believe he'd sunk low enough to call a 900 number.

Once.

Jamal turned the car off, pumped the gas pedal, and then turned the key in the ignition again. The churning was worse than before, giving no hint of turning over, making him think he'd flooded the engine—though, what did he know? Cars were not his game. Now, ask him whether Microsoft was out-performing Apple and he could quote figures that would make a stockbroker's mind spin.

Unfortunately, the figures that he was so passionate about made the mind of just about everyone else spin. Not in a good way.

Jamal yanked the keys from the ignition and picked up his cell phone to call a cab. It was dead. "Fuck!"

But all was not lost.

Forty-five minutes later, the cab he'd called from a pay phone after walking along the freeway to the nearest exit, pulled up in front of the Marriott Hotel to drop him off.

What were the odds that Sharice would still be waiting an hour later, even if she had received his message he'd left from the pay phone informing her that he was running late?

Jamal passed through the lobby and up the escalator to the second floor. The brightly lit bar, which catered more to business travelers than locals, was almost deserted except for a couple of suits talking around a table in the corner and the woman at the bar.

Her back was to him but what he could see was inspiring. The smooth caramel shoulders revealed by the black halter-top tied at her neck were kissable, the small waist molded by the tight material was grippable, and the round hips and even rounder ass atop the stool made him want to pull her off the stool and onto his lap. Damn. The things he could do with that. He let his gaze drift lower, to the shapely legs, crossed at the ankle, and the two-inch heeled sandals on her feet.

Daaaaamn.

The image of those legs wrapped around his waist flashed through his mind, the tips of those sandals poking his ass as he thrust forward, pumping hard, gripping those hips—

His cock twitched.

He cursed, forcing his mind to focus on the mundane, like each step that he took to reach the bar. Like what he was going to say when he got there. He stopped at the vacant barstool next to her, inhaling a faint flowery scent wafting from skin that looked even more touchable, squeezable, kissable than it did twenty feet away.

She was fine, in a Beyoncé kind of way—which was not the kind of woman he dated. Ultra-fine women tended to be divas and divas tended to be high maintenance and materialistic, going for the showy brothas fronting in their Lexes and Jags. A serious, studious-looking man driving a dilapidated hoopdie didn't register in their consciousness—even if this type had a financial portfolio a hundred times more solid than their flashy counterparts. Or so he'd heard from both Byron and King, who dated only divas.

So what was he doing here?

Satisfying his curiosity. Saving a stranger from the clutches of a dog.

Yeah, right.

Jamal slid onto the stool. The woman gave no awareness of his presence, didn't say, *I'm sorry. I'm waiting for someone.* Which could mean that she'd given up on Shawn. Or that she wasn't Sharice

"Hi, I'm . . ." *Shawn* ". . . Jamal. Are you—"

The question evaporated from his mind as she raised her head and turned to him, facing him head on. A slow burning fire seemed to simmer within her brown eyes, as if she were on her back, under him, waiting for him to fill her, instead of in this near-empty room. Her glossy lips were parted, as if waiting for his lips to possess hers in a kiss that plundered and demanded.

His heart drummed.

His breath hung.

His cock surged.

For the first time in months, Jamal desired a woman more than a column of numbers on a performance statement.

Her shapely, succulent lips quirked in a smile. "No, I'm not."

Those three words throbbed with sexiness, curling around his cock, confirming that she was the woman he'd spoken to on the phone.

He raised a brow, happy to feel his eyebrows were still functional. "You're not . . .?"

"No, I'm not with anyone. No, I'm not married. No, I'm not expecting anyone . . ."

Jamal forced his mind from the hypnotic purr of her voice to her words. Alright, another question answered. She'd given up on Shawn. Smart woman.

Her tongue caressed her lower lip. ". . . well, I'm not expecting anyone *anymore.*"

He gave himself a mental shake. Time to get his

cool back on. "Maybe I wasn't going to ask any of those things."

"You were."

With forced casualness, he asked, "Why do you say that?"

The smile still curved her lips as she raised her glass, placed it against lips that he wanted to taste. He watched her throat ripple as she swallowed, suppressing the urge to lean forward and press his lips against her neck, tracing her throat with his tongue.

Suddenly, he was jealous of a glass of ice cubes.

"You stood in the doorway and stared at me, debating whether or not to come over and say something."

How had she seen him? His gaze left hers briefly, taking in the mirrored surface covering the back of the bar, behind the hanging glasses. He hadn't noticed them before. Mystery solved. "Yeah, I did stare at you but that wasn't what I was debating."

She tipped her glass and inclined her head slightly. "Oh?"

No. I was watching the light on your skin, making it shine, making me want to run my tongue along a shoulder to see if you tasted salty or sweet or both, before—

Forget that shit. Get to the point. Tell her you're not Shawn.

But maybe he didn't need to mention Shawn. After all, *she* didn't think he was Shawn.

"No. I knew I was going to come over to you. I was debating what to say when I got here."

"Honesty's a refreshing trait." She took another sip of her drink. Watching her the second time had the same effect it did the first time. Jamal licked his lips, wishing it was his cock—instead of the alcohol—

entering her mouth, feeling the hot wetness caressing him, before moving to the back of her throat, feeling its tightness—

"Tell me, Jamal. Are you single?"

He blinked, returning his focus to the present. The glass was back on the black bar top, her fingertip circling the lip of the glass.

"Yes."

"Do you date a lot?"

"Enough."

Her laughter tickled his eardrums, causing a vibration to throb through his body and tighten the invisible hold she already had on his cock. It twitched again, harder this time.

"That's funny?" he asked.

"Your tone implies that you don't like dating."

"I don't." He forced a nonchalant shrug he was far from feeling. "The games. The posturing. It gets old real quick."

She nodded, though whether in agreement he couldn't tell. His gaze was drawn to her pink-tipped fingernail, tracing the rim of a tumbler.

"What are you drinking?" he asked.

"A Dirty Minnie."

"A Dirty Minnie? What's in that?"

"Stoli Strasberi, Vodka, Amaretto, Grenadine . . ." she shrugged ". . . and more."

Damn. "Strong stuff . . . May I buy you another one?"

"Thank you, but I've had enough."

Her finger kept circling the glass. The movement hypnotized, taking his mind back to the heels digging into his ass, and those fingertips gripping his shoulders to hold on before slipping to his back,

13

squeezing and tracing his shoulders while her pussy squeezed and stroked his cock.

He interrupted the direction of his thoughts in disgust. What the fuck was wrong with him? He was acting like the dog he'd accused Shawn of being. He'd come here just to satisfy his curiosity.

His curiosity was satisfied.

He hadn't come here to pick her up, to take Shawn's place.

But he wanted to pick her up; he wanted to take Shawn's place. Despite the fact that he never picked up women in bars. Despite the fact that he steered clear of divas. Only, so far, he hadn't gotten the impression she was a diva. She didn't sound high-maintenance and demanding but . . .

How did he know what she was or was not? He knew nothing about her—though his cock was desperate to make her acquaintance.

That was another thing he never did: Let his cock lead the show—outside of the bedroom, that is. Jamal was always the epitome of control and reason, choosing women based on suitability criteria, of which sexual attraction was only one part—

"Have you ever stood a woman up?"

Ah, Shit.

"No." Enough. It was time to tell her. "Listen,—"

"Would you stand *me* up, Jamal?"

The breathy sound of his name from her lips turned his mouth to cotton. Jamal swallowed hard, summoning moisture. "Uh, no."

Her full, sexy lips quirked into a half-smile. "Right answer." The pink fingernail he'd watched trace the glass, moved to trace the same circles on his hand.

His cock jerked.

"Since you'd never stand me up, what would you like to do right now? With me?"

Her finger moved along his wrist, swirling along the sensitive skin, sending prickles up his arm and quivers through his cock.

Her voice said she knew exactly what he wanted.

Her skin moving against his skin, firing up his body and searing all thoughts from his mind, told him what she wanted the answer to be.

He opened his mouth to give her his answer. The right answer.

3

Sharice watched Jamal's full lips part, as if he were going to say something, then close, as if he'd changed his mind. She stared into his brown eyes, keeping her gaze flirtatious and masking her anxiety. But she was operating on automatic pilot, going through the motions of being playful and sexy, while feeling anything but.

Unlike past appearances on the pick-up scene, she cared about the outcome to this one—cared if Jamal wasn't interested. Maybe because his chest didn't puff up—as if he'd just won the prize of the day, seeing her as a prize for his ego, instead of a woman with needs of her own—when she'd let him know she was attracted to him. Or maybe it was because he'd stared at her for a good few minutes before coming over to her, as if he were working up the courage to do so.

Though Lord only knew—with his maple-syrup eyes that had stolen her breath when she'd looked up at him; his sexy mouth that she'd like to trace with her finger before, during, and after she kissed him; and his shaved head that she'd love to run her hands over—why he'd felt the need to work up the courage. He surely got his share of female attention.

She moved her fingers higher, trailing over his forearm and up to his biceps. "Maybe you'd like to . . ."

She squeezed his biceps lightly, liking the firmness, liking the fact that he didn't just look muscular, he *was* muscular. She moved beyond his shoulder, trailing her fingertips inside his collar, caressing the chocolaty skin above it. Chocolaty skin that she was dying to taste, lick, suck.

". . . get to . . . know each other better?"

Jamal's eyes flared. "How much better?"

Sharice smiled, moving her fingers up his neck to his chin, flicking them along his lower lip. Softly tracing. Lightly touching. "Intimately better. Tonight, I want to get to know every inch of you. One night. No . . . complications."

Jamal's eyes darkened. "Are you sure you want that with *me?*"

Sharice licked her lower lip and dipped her finger inside Jamal's mouth. "Is there a reason why I shouldn't want that with you, Jamal?"

He moved his head back slightly so that Sharice's finger grazed his inner lip. His tongue appeared between his lips. He licked.

Sharice suppressed a gasp, a jolt of lust clenching her stomach at Jamal's sleepy gaze and liquid touch. He lifted his hand, wrapped his fingers around hers, and pulled her hand back. Brushing his lips across her knuckles, he produced another barely restrained shiver through her.

"Wait here," he said, giving her hand a squeeze

before placing it back on the counter.

Watching him slide from the stool and walk to the exit, Sharice was pleased by the way his jeans hugged his ass.

God, what was she doing? She'd never before said just a handful of words to a guy and then invited him to bed. The fun was making it long and leisurely. Like dancing close enough to feel the man's body heat caressing her skin, the occasional stroke of knee against thigh, the narrowed gaze stealing a hot glance down the "v" of her dress when he thought she wasn't looking, or watching her body move in sync with his as they danced, hips rotating and gyrating mere inches apart, mimicking private acts where hips and skin touched. The fun was in the teasing, in becoming so aroused that clothes were shed almost before the door of his place had closed, he was inside her before they made it to a bed, and it was over before it got started. The foreplay happened on the dance floor; the sex happened behind closed doors; and she could leave, satisfied. A passionate encounter that sparked immediately and was extinguished quickly. Since she was already aroused before sex, the guy didn't have to have a stellar technique to bring her to orgasm.

But she and Jamal had barely talked.

They'd barely touched.

There'd been no foreplay.

A tight body, sexy eyes, and a promising touch did not guarantee a satisfying sexual experience. While she felt aroused, she was a long way from pre-orgasmic. Which meant, depending on his technique, she might be stuck behind closed doors with him longer than usual. Which might lead to awkwardness.

Awkwardness, like expectations of getting to know each other nonsexually.

So why had she propositioned him?

Jamal was back in front of her before she had the answer.

And she'd slipped her hand into his hand, slid off the stool, darted into the elevator, and was standing in front of a hotel room before she had a chance to change her mind.

As Jamal opened the door and led her into the room, her mouth dropped open.

He'd rented a suite.

To the right was a sitting area with a plush couch and matching chair. Behind that was a dining area, with a tall circular table and tall black chairs. A bar and a kitchenette with black granite countertops rounded out the room.

Unease skittered up her back. A suite seemed a bit too elaborate for a one-night stand. Sharice looked beyond Jamal's shoulder, caught a glimpse of where he was leading her, and tugged his hand, stopping him.

He turned back, his brow lifted in inquiry.

Sharice sidled up to him, smiling seductively—or so she hoped, for she suddenly felt nervous. She didn't want him to lead her to the bedroom. She wanted to get the party started here, in the living room, now. Preferably, against a wall or across the couch.

Somehow, the bedroom seemed too intimate.

Pressing herself against him, she slid her hands up his back, to his neck, to the back of his head, where she pulled him to her, lowering his head. His lips touched hers, soft and firm at the same time. Soft in feel, but firm in what they wanted—to taste, to explore.

He took control of the kiss, ending her teasing nibbles, parting her lips and thrusting inside. His hand cupped her head, guiding her to where he wanted her to be, controlling the pressure.

His tongue met hers, then retreated.

Her tongue explored his, then retreated.

Advancing and withdrawing, lips and mouths fought for dominance.

Sharice moved her hand restlessly over his back, sliding under the cotton shirt to feel flesh. Smooth, muscular flesh.

A gasp escaped her. Jamal swallowed it, his lips pressing harder against hers, his tongue probing deeper, demanding more.

She moved her hips against his, feeling his cock jerk against her pelvis.

A thrill of power thrummed through her, stoking the lust that was welling up inside her. He was hot. She was hot. This was about sex.

To prove the point, Sharice moved her hands along his waist, dipping under the waistband of his jeans.

His skin quivered.

She slid her hands to the front, fumbling for the button, unsnapping, unzipping.

Jamal inhaled sharply before moving her hands away. He drew away.

Sharice opened her dazed eyes and looked into his. "Change your mind?" Her tone was supposed to be teasing. It echoed with traces of pleading instead.

He smiled. A sexy, heavy-lidded smile that told her his mind was in sync with his cock.

She pulled him toward her again.

He pulled away, stepping back. "I want to take a shower."

Sharice blinked, her mind attempting to focus on his words. She couldn't remember the last time a guy had pulled away to go shower—well, maybe after a hot workout session on the couch or floor or both of the above. She resisted the urge to turn her head and do a quick smell test.

"Okay," she lied. It wasn't okay. She didn't want to stop.

Still wearing the smile, Jamal turned, keeping hold of her hands and pulling her along behind him into the bathroom.

Oh. He meant he wanted them to take a shower *together.*

A frisson of discomfort bubbled in her stomach. She hadn't taken a shower with a man since Darrell. There'd been candles and champagne, which they hadn't touched until afterward, so anxious they'd been to fuck.

Only, it hadn't been just a fuck—or so she'd thought, until she'd walked in on the same scene with him and her best friend weeks later. It didn't take a doctorate degree to know that he just wasn't that "into" her.

She stopped in front of the sink, causing Jamal to turn back to her.

She tried to remove her hand from his grasp.

He held tight.

"You go ahead. I'll shower after you," she said.

"Hmmm." Jamal released her hands, sliding them up her arms, his gaze following their action, as if there was something interesting to their movement. Trailing her shoulders, they circled inward, tracing the neckline of her top, to the hint of cleavage.

Her skin prickled under his path.

Her breath hitched, though whether from the touch of his fingers or the intense way he stared at her body as if memorizing every line, she didn't know.

His fingertip dipped into the valley between her breasts, before moving down. Both hands rested on her waist.

"You want to take a shower alone?" he asked, his hands lightly stroking her waist.

No. "Yeah."

He stared at her, his dark eyes taking in her eyes, before moving to her lips, lingering. When his gaze returned to hers, his eyes resembled melted Belgian chocolate.

Hot. Wet. Gooey.

"Okay," he said, sliding his hands under the hem of her dress, over the outside of her thighs and hips, and up the sides of her body.

Sharice shivered, unable to stop herself.

"Lift your arms."

"What are you doing?"

"Getting you ready for your shower."

Sharice laughed, suddenly self-conscious. It was one thing to undress while caught up in the moment, but . . . under the harsh fluorescent lighting while in the midst of a nonsexual conversation, well, that felt . . .

"Shy?"

Sharice laughed again. "No." And it was true. She didn't have a shy bone where her body was concerned. No, Jamal made her feel off-balance. Things were happening that shouldn't be happening.

Fast and furious sex wasn't happening like it was supposed to. Shit, forget about fast and furious sex— *nothing* was happening yet.

If nothing is happening, why are you tripping?

Jamal tugged on her shirt. "Up."

Sharice shrugged off the question and lifted her arms.

Her dress came off.

Her bra sprung apart as Jamal unhooked it.

He paused, his gaze roving her breasts. "Beautiful," he whispered, skimming a fingertip over the swell of her breast before lowering his head.

Sharice held her breath.

His lips grazed the top of her breasts, kissing lightly, softly, before he withdrew.

Nooooooo . . .

Sharice suppressed a groan, forcing herself to remain still, not giving in to the urge to grab his head and guide it to the nipples that had hardened, despite the fact that he hadn't touched them. Nipples that strained for his touch and tongue, despite that fact that he had neither stroked nor licked them.

Jamal drew back, his hands dropping to her waist, slipping under the waistband of her panties, before drawing them down over her hips. They fell silently to the floor.

Jamal stood silently, staring. His hands rested on either side of her lower hips. "Beautiful," he said again, his voice barely above a strained whisper. His hands moved inward.

Sharice gasped.

His thumbs lightly caressed the lips that pulsed with need, beating and throbbing, as if her heart had suddenly landed there.

She tilted her hips upward, guiding his fingers to where she wanted them, begging him with her body to separate her pussy lips, and stroke her lightly, then slightly harder. Slow, then faster.

Instead, Jamal moved his hands over her hips and took a step back. "Since you want to shower alone, you can watch me."

With one smooth movement, his polo shirt was over his head and on the floor.

Sharice watched muscled biceps and toned abs with lustful eyes.

In a second smooth movement, the button on his jeans was undone, his zipper was unzipped, and briefs and jeans slid over lean hips.

Sharice watched the muscles in his thighs clench as he stepped out of the circle of his clothes, watched his cock jerk upward, straining toward her, as he straightened again. "If you'd like to join me at any time . . ."

With a half-smile, he turned, threw the shower curtain back and leaned over the faucet.

Sharice leaned back against the sink, feeling weak-kneed at the sight of two perfectly toned ass cheeks. God, did this man have an ounce of flab anywhere on his body? The jeans and baggy shirt had hinted at muscles but . . . damn. Most guys with a body like Jamal's would be flaunting it, not hiding it behind loose clothing.

Water gushed out of the showerhead. Jamal tore open the package of soap, grabbed a wash cloth, and stepped into the tub. Leaving the curtain open, he turned to face her and lathered up the wash cloth, then moved away from the spray of water.

His hand brushed an arm, shoulder, and chest,

before repeating the action on the other side.

White soapy foam bubbled on his mocha skin.

Sharice swallowed hard, summoning moisture for her parched throat.

Jamal reached behind him, soaping up his back.

Sharice resisted the urge to do it for him.

His hands returned to the front, running over his chest and abs and hips and—

Sharice groaned.

—Cock.

The cloth hid his cock for a second, before he tossed it aside. His hands stroked it. "It would be a shame to waste this." His voice was husky.

Yes, it would be a damn shame.

Jamal's hand pumped, sliding over and around the head of his penis, then back down.

Sharice's heart pumped, pushing the blood through her, pooling it between her legs, where her pussy still throbbed and pulsed in sync with her heart.

It's time to sin. Dr. Love's words rang through her head.

He was right. She'd been sinning ever since she took the initiative and called Shawn. Why stop now? Why should she fight the delectable specimen in front of her, flexing muscles she couldn't wait to touch, stroking a cock she couldn't wait to feel inside her?

She didn't want to stop. Didn't want to worry about the past or the future. No sense in letting it ruin what appeared to be a perfectly good shower fuck.

Is that all that's going on here, a shower fuck?

Sharice ignored the question and pushed away from the sink. She walked toward the shower and stepped inside. She let her gaze run the length of Jamal as her hand circled his cock.

He jerked in her hand. The breath exploded from his lips, bouncing off of her neck.

Sharice pumped her hand, loving his smooth hardness. Her heart raced. Her breath shook. "No, I definitely do not want this to go to waste." Her voice was shaky.

With one hand on her shoulder, he guided her under the flow of the water. With the other, he wrapped his hand around hers and stopped her ministrations to his cock.

"You don't like that?" she asked.

"I love that. But first things first." He reached back, grabbed a clean cloth from the rack and lathered it with soap. His hands glided over her neck and shoulders, down the front of her arms and up the backside, to her side, across her stomach, to the undersides of her breasts.

There was nothing overtly sexual about the touch, but Sharice's nerve endings sparked with arousal.

There was nothing about the cloth rubbing along her skin that should have made her feel tense, but she did. The fact that Jamal watched the progress of the white cotton caressing her skin, coupled with the palms of his hands that followed, smoothing the soap bubbles along her flesh, as if he had all the time in the world, as if this was enough for him, as if this was not leading to the fuck that she imagined.

That was what made her uncomfortable.

His actions were intentional. As if he knew her need to hurry but wanted to keep it slow, drawing it out, making it last longer than it should.

Sharice wanted to move, to reach out and squeeze the cock that still reached for her, that still beckoned to her hand, to spur him on.

But she didn't.

Instead, she stood still, marveling at the sense of vulnerability that she thought she'd long ago lost, awestruck by Jamal's enjoyment of her body in a way she couldn't remember anyone enjoying her body ever. Not Malcolm. Not Darrell. Not any of the casual sex partners after them.

Jamal's touch and his intense gaze combined to make what should feel like a fuck, feel like making love, thereby turning what she thought was making love with Malcolm and Darrell into fucks.

They hadn't treated her body with this reverence, this admiration. They hadn't treated her body with love.

But Jamal was.

Her head spun with the realization.

Jamal's hands, spreading soap over her breasts, sent her head spinning for an entirely different reason.

She gasped.

He smiled, moving his hand down her ribcage and over her abdomen, stopping at the bottom, where her stomach gave way to pelvis, and pelvis led to pussy, which lead to—

Sharice pressed into his hand.

Jamal moved his hand to her hip, holding her still, while using the other one to drag the washcloth over her hips, to her ass, then back to her thighs.

"I didn't know you were sadistic," she said, her voice trembly.

"I'm not."

"Oh? Then this slow torture is supposed to be pleasurable?"

He smeared soap over her thighs, his fingertips

grazing her swollen lips.

"It would be . . ." His finger dipped inside.

Sharice stumbled.

". . . If you let yourself feel it."

Oh, she was going to feel it all right. His finger was where she wanted it. Finally.

"Are you going to feel it?"

"Yes."

"Good. Because I want you to feel it. I want you to feel me."

One second, he was standing and the next he was kneeling before her, his gaze riveted to the spot where his finger explored. Moving his hand higher, he used his fingers to pull her pussy lips up and apart. He leaned forward. His lips touched her pussy in a light kiss. His tongue dipped between her lips, giving her one . . . long . . . lick.

Oh. God.

"Like that?" he asked, his breath heating her already inflamed pussy.

"Yessss."

"I like it, too." He lapped again. And again. And again.

Sharice fell back against the wall, letting her head loll back and her eyes half close. Her nails raked the slick tiled wall of the shower, grasping for purchase that was not there. The water poured from the spigot, pounding in her ears, hitting her shoulders and side, bouncing off of her body, off the walls, and off the tub.

Jamal's tongue stroked.

Sharice's legs trembled. Fire pooled in her stomach, spilling over, spreading out, climbing higher.

Jamal gripped her hips, both guiding her and

supporting her, as his tongue drove her higher, leaving her breathless, panting, wanting, needing.

Sharice held his head, which felt smooth and wet, using her hands to ask for more pressure, first guiding, then caressing.

He got it. His laps were faster and harder, longer and deeper.

She tried to hang on to the feeling, to suppress the crescendo of sensation, to make it last.

But she couldn't. Jamal wouldn't let her. Sharice let out a cry when orgasm burst from her hold.

Sensation slammed through her.

She moaned.

Her legs buckled.

Dropping her hands to his shoulders, she gripped the hard muscle to keep herself upright.

Jamal's licks became soft kisses, no longer caressing her sensitive clit, instead caressing her outer lips.

As the last shudder faded from her body, she became aware of the water beating on her, beating on Jamal, beading on his smooth skull and his buff shoulders before rolling off.

Awe replaced arousal.

Shock replaced sensation.

While she enjoyed oral sex, Sharice had never orgasmed from it. Oh, she'd pretended to, when the guy she was with tried real hard. But she'd rarely been able to let go, namely because the guys she'd let do it seemed to do it because it was expected, not because they seemed to enjoy it. They gave her clit and pussy about twenty seconds of attention, before whipping out their cocks and plunging in.

Which was fine with her, since she managed to

come anyway.

But Jamal hadn't stopped. Jamal hadn't come yet.

Jamal hadn't seemed to kiss and lick her because it was expected. In fact, it was the opposite. She hadn't asked for it. Jamal seemed to have done it because he'd wanted to. Because he desired her—and wanted her to desire it, too.

And she had let go. She hadn't had to force unwanted thoughts from her mind. She didn't have any thoughts in her mind. Just feeling. Just sensation. Just pleasure.

And she'd come. Why?

She didn't want to think about why he'd been the first to make her come this way. She didn't want to think about why not once had she thought about this as a fuck.

She didn't want to think about why—

Jamal rose, placed his hands on her shoulders and turned her toward the wall. The wet tile chilled her cheek. His chest pressed against her back. His cock jerked against her ass. "My God. I can't believe how beautiful you are."

His hands dropped to her hips, gripping.

His breath hit her neck, heating.

His teeth nipped her shoulder, biting.

Jamal grabbed her hands, holding them above her head against the tile, while rubbing his hips against her ass, his cock probing the entrance to her pussy. "Is this what you want?" he demanded.

The arousal that had been replaced by awe zoomed through her again.

The sensation that had been replaced by shock jolted her.

This she was familiar with. This she could handle.

"Yes, that's what I want."

He ran his lips over her shoulder, stopping at the sensitive spot no one before had ever discovered. He licked hard. He sucked hard. Heat sparked her pussy.

"What do you want?" he rasped.

"I want—"

His cock entered her pussy, pausing after only the head was covered.

Sharice moaned. "I want you to fuck me."

Jamal laughed. "Yeah, I know—that's what you *think* you want."

His cock slid into her another inch.

Sharice gasped.

"But *I* think you want . . ."

And another inch.

Sharice jutted her hips back.

". . . This." Jamal caught her mouth with his and slowly pressed his hips forward at the same time.

His cock filled her pussy.

His tongue filled her mouth.

Sharice moaned.

Jamal swallowed her moan. His tongue slowly circled—grazing her teeth, the roof of her mouth, before suckling her tongue. Exploring thoroughly, moving purposely, as if savoring every taste, memorizing every crevice.

She craned her neck further back, seeking to taste more of him.

She pressed her hips back, attempting to feel more of him.

Jamal moved away, withdrawing his cock, then moved forward, burying his cock. His hands released hers and gripped her hips, holding her still, forcing her to endure the excruciatingly slow pace.

He broke his mouth from hers, trailing his tongue along her cheek, to her earlobe.

He nipped.

She shivered.

"This . . ." he whispered, dotting her jaw with feathery kisses. He moved his hips back, leaving only the tip of his cock inside.

". . . is what . . ."

He licked her neck lightly and moved his hips forward, inching into her slowly.

". . . you want . . ."

He kissed her neck tenderly and ground his hips against her ass, rotating one direction, then the other.

"Isn't it?" he breathed into her ear.

Desire that Sharice thought he'd satisfied with his tongue, flared from his cock.

His hands slid from her hips, over her ass, and between her legs to her lips, spreading them, zeroing in on her clit.

He rubbed.

She climbed.

His hips remained unmoving, locked in place, pressing her flat against the tile. Sharice was imprisoned between the wall and him, unable to move, forced to remain motionless.

He jerked his cock rhythmically inside her pussy, the sensation magnified by his still body.

She clenched her muscles, holding him tight inside her.

"Tell me this is what you want. My touch. My desire. My kiss. All of me."

He twitched.

She gripped.

His fingertips danced along her flesh, making her

dizzy, making her breathless, making her aware of nothing but him. His body . . . his fingers . . .

"Tell me."

. . . his words.

But she couldn't tell him in words. Instead, her body quaked, her legs trembled, and heat once again exploded inside her, speeding her heart, consuming her breath, and forcing a cry from her throat.

The seconds ticked by in silence. She couldn't speak. Wouldn't speak.

Finally, the room came back into focus. Sharice became aware of the heat from Jamal's body, tense and rigid against hers; the hardness of his cock still resting inside her, while the cold seeped into her breasts, stomach, and thighs from the wet tiles she was pressed against. The water hitting her had also gone from comfortable heat to barely lukewarm.

Sharice shivered.

"You couldn't even bring yourself to say it, could you?" His voice was soft.

His words hurt her ears.

"You wanted this . . ." His cock, still hard, jerked inside her. ". . . and you wanted me . . ." His mouth moved over hers, softly, gently, tenderly, as if her lips were fragile.

She couldn't kiss him back.

"Why can't you admit it?"

It was fitting that the water suddenly turned from lukewarm to cold. It matched her insides for she felt cold—frigid, even—inside. She couldn't admit it because . . . she'd felt empty for so long. She'd become comfortable with that emptiness because she didn't have to feel, didn't have to want, didn't have to hurt. Jamal was asking her to let go of that emptiness, to let him in. And the thought of doing that turned her insides to ice.

Jamal kissed her cheek lightly and withdrew from her, then moved away. She heard him turn the water off and pull open the shower curtain. She turned away from the wall, just in time to see his outstretched hand with the towel.

"Thank you," she said, taking it with a small smile but not looking at him.

Awkwardness had set in. She felt awkward because something had happened that wasn't supposed to happen. Whether or not she wanted to admit it, Jamal was right. She had wanted more. For once, she wasn't just feeling body parts licking, kissing, and entering her. Despite being caught up in the sensations he'd caused to swirl within her, she'd been aware of the man attached to the sensations. She'd felt a connection to him.

Sharice did not do "connections."

She toweled dry hurriedly, then stepped out of the shower, and reached down to pick up her clothes.

Jamal grabbed her hand, which brought her eyes to his. "Stay," he said.

"I can't."

Because if she did, she might want to stay longer. Then she'd want to see him again. And before she knew it, she'd be calling in to *The Sin Club* telling Dr. Love that she wanted a relationship. But, unlike Jessie, her foray into the relationship arena would not end happily.

It never did.

"You can't stay—or you won't?"

Sharice's attention turned back to Jamal. "Can't" implied that there was something preventing her from staying, while "won't" implied free choice, a mere decision not to do something.

Sharice's sense of panic around staying did not feel like free will.

"I can't."

Jamal's hand drifted up her arm, stroking and persuading. "What are you afraid of?"

"I'm not afraid of anything." *Liar.* "Look, it was great—you were great—but I don't do the strings thing."

"I'm not asking you for 'strings.' I'm just asking you to stay the night. Sleep with me in a bed. Let me make love to you in a bed."

Make love.

The words sent an unwanted rush of pleasure through her veins while simultaneously causing her stomach to turn. She gently removed her grasp from his. "I'm sorry, Jamal. And I'm sorry that you didn't get to . . ." *come* ". . . finish . . . I feel really bad about that—"

"Then stay."

"I have to go." She stretched forward and brushed a kiss against his lips. His unmoving lips. She walked away from him and quickly dressed.

Still not looking at him, she picked up her purse.

"Thanks," she said lamely and walked out the door.

~~~~

Jamal stared at the door, resisting the urge to smash his hand against it. What the fuck had just happened? Minutes ago, he'd been holding the most delectable ass, his body rubbing against the softest skin he could remember feeling, drugged by the scent of soap and woman and need, his cock harder than he could remember, her pussy gripping him so tightly he'd wanted to pump into her forever.

And he hadn't been the only one into it. He'd felt her body vibrate with desire, shudder when he'd made her come with his mouth. And he'd felt her spasm around him when he'd been inside her, which had sent his need spiraling upward, his come spiraling outward—

Your come didn't spiral outward.

Shit.

He reached down to pick up his briefs from the floor, then paused. His briefs would have to wait a minute, wait until he erased all thought of Sharice's wild response to his body, his touch, his tongue—

Damn, she had tasted good. Like—

His cock surged.

He yanked his briefs over his hips, glad for the discomfort, the perfect punishment for standing here, mooning over some woman who obviously didn't want him.

And why didn't she want him? Because, instead of giving her the fuck she'd wanted, he'd said all that wimpy shit about what *he* wanted her to want. He'd done shit that left him feeling weak, shit that women supposedly wanted—like, want men to want them, need them, take care of them. That's what he'd tried to do for Sharice. But it'd been the wrong approach with the wrong woman.

Maybe if he'd been the smooth "playa" type he suspected Shawn of being, she'd still be with him right now—in bed, making that come-inspiring sound in the back of her throat, panting and writhing with need under him, while he held himself off of her, staring into her heavy eyes, taking in her parted lips, as he thrust inside her, watching her eyes lose focus as the turmoil he was causing in her body forced her to notice only what her body was feeling, what he was making her feel, what—

His cock, which had been starting to go down, returned to its granite state.

Jamal yanked his jeans from the floor and put them on.

Well, he wasn't Shawn. Though, for one split second, he wished he was. Because Shawn wouldn't have demanded more than she wanted to give. Wouldn't have wanted more than she wanted. Wouldn't have made her feel trapped, because the last thing a playa wants is a trap.

And, most importantly, Shawn wouldn't be standing here thinking about her after she'd walked out the door.

4

A couple hours later, Sharice sat in her car, staring out over Lake Merritt with her cell phone in her hand. Since leaving Jamal, she'd driven around aimlessly, not wanting to go home. What would she do there? She wasn't sleepy and she was too restless to watch a movie or read a book. She didn't even feel like clubbing—something that seemed to be happening more and more frequently.

So, she'd driven South on I-880 for over an hour, then turned around and headed back home to Oakland. Instead of going to her townhouse, she'd stopped at the lake. All the while, she'd been thinking—thinking about how to get rid of the panic Jamal had inspired. The last few years, she'd been happy being footloose and fancy-free. Not once had she wished for a connection with some man.

Until tonight.

Why? Just because he'd made her come in a way no man had before?

No.

The connection had started before that, had started down in the bar, when he'd approached her. He'd almost seemed vulnerable—not like the practiced men she was used to meeting. She'd been drawn to him, despite the fact that he hadn't issued one smooth line, made one empty compliment.

Which was a big reason for the attraction. Which was a big reason for her discomfort. Because, somehow, he seemed to see beneath the surface to the things she wanted to hide. Which made her feel . . . vulnerable.

Well, you know what to do when you feel vulnerable.

Run away from things, that's what.

"I am not running away."

Yes, you are.

Sharice frowned. No, she wasn't. She just knew what she didn't want. She didn't want a connection, which could lead to the desire for a relationship, which would lead to heartbreak.

Been there, done that.

Maybe Jamal is different.

Sharice snorted and flipped open her cell phone. Yeah, right. Enough of this thinking. The only way to get rid of these thoughts was to get back on track, to go for the one-night kind of man she'd been looking for. Well, not tonight. Jamal had left her more than satisfied. No, now she'd just set something up for . . . soon.

To wipe away the memory of Jamal.

She dialed the number that had started this whole mess with Jamal, holding little hope that it'd be answered at 3:47 A.M. While the phone rang, she stared at the light from the streetlights reflecting off the water.

Shawn answered on the second ring, taking her by surprise. "Oh. Hi, Shawn, this is Sharice."

A slight pause. "Hi, Sharice."

His voice sounded . . . funny. Deeper and huskier than last time. Of course, the last time, the connection had been so bad, she could barely hear him. Now he sounded clear.

She said, "Did I call at a bad time?"

"I got a minute."

"I got that message you left earlier, but there was a lot of static so I couldn't make it out. Were you calling to make it up to me for standing me up?"

"Then, I was calling to tell you I had car problems. Now, I'm . . ." He paused then continued, ". . . offering to make it up."

"Oh? And what are you going to do to make it up to me?" she asked, forcing a teasing playfulness to her tone.

Another pause, then, "I'm going to give you what you wanted when you . . . called me."

"A drink, Shawn?" she asked with mock innocence, injecting a purr to her voice she didn't really feel.

What was wrong with her? Why did she feel . . . empty, like she was watching herself go through the motions from a distance, without really feeling anything?

He laughed, his laugh reminding her of Jamal's.

She suppressed a snort of disgust. She was *not going* to think of Jamal. She *was going* to get into this with Shawn.

"Where are you?" he asked, changing the subject.

Parked at Lake Merritt, trying not to think. "In my

car."

"What are you doing now?"

Trying to forget about Jamal. "Sitting here, talking to you."

"What are you wearing?" Shawn's voice took on a raspy sound.

Sharice's laugh sounded forced to her own ears. "This is starting to sound like phone sex."

"It is." The huskiness in his voice reminded her of Jamal. The way Jamal had sounded when he'd slipped his finger into her pussy and told her it'd feel good if she let it.

And it had felt *sooooo* good as he'd dipped and swirled, rubbed and stroked—

A flash of arousal zipped through her—the first one she'd felt since she'd made the phone call.

Phone sex.

Right. She could do that. She'd never done it before, but she could do it. Replace thoughts of Jamal with thoughts of . . . what was his name? The guy on the phone?

Shawn.

Right. Shawn. What had he asked her? Oh yeah, what was she wearing. "Okay. I'm wearing—"

"Black."

"How'd you know that?"

"Because black is my favorite color."

Sharice's laugh felt a little more natural. "Okay. What are you wearing?"

"Jeans."

Jamal had been wearing jeans. "Button fly or zipper?"

"Zipper." Like Jamal's.

Oh, for God's sake, 99 percent of men have jeans with

zippers.

To get herself and the conversation back on track, she said, "If I asked you to unzip your jeans right now, would you?"

"Yes."

"Okay. Do it."

"Okay . . . I did it."

Like Jamal had done it—unzipped his jeans, hooked his fingers underneath the waistband of the denim and his briefs, the movement of his hands taking her breath with the material as his flesh was bared before her eyes. Mouthwatering thighs, fantasy-inducing cock . . .

"Are you hard?" she asked.

"Do you want me to be?"

"Yes . . ."

Jamal had been hard before he'd even touched himself, had been rigid with need by the time she'd wrapped her hands around him. And yet, he'd taken his time, seemingly having no desire to rush.

"Okay . . . I imagined you touching me. I'm hard." Shawn's voice sounded strained.

Like Jamal's had been when he'd asked her to stay, to make love with him in the bed.

"Good. Because I am touching you, . . ." *Jamal* ". . . Shawn. I'm running my fingertips down the length of your cock, over the head, then skimming the underside, before taking you in my hand and . . ."

Sharice saw herself with Jamal—as she would have been if she hadn't left Jamal in the bed in the hotel room. She would be naked. He would be naked. She would push him back into the pillows, his dark head adding beautiful color to the white linen. She would straddle him, his cock resting between the folds of her pussy, pressing up against her clit. She would move her hips against his, creating friction that would send delicious tingles radiating from where their flesh touched. Her movements would become frenzied, demanding, needing the release that hovered . . . right . . . in . . . her—

". . . and . . .?" prompted Shawn, bringing her attention back to him.

She told Shawn that she pumped his cock with her hand, loving the way it felt, imagining how it would feel inside her, filling her.

But her mind pictured Jamal's cock, returned to the image of Jamal beneath her, of an orgasm rocking her as she rocked against him. She imagined crying out his name, seconds before their positions were switched and she was underneath him.

Shawn whispered her name, causing Jamal's image to evaporate.

Heavy breathing echoed over the phone seconds before she heard Shawn's muttered curse.

His release caressed her eardrums.

Her tension grew, her own release trapped within, wanting to come out. But not with Shawn. *Oh, Jamal,* she thought, imagining his lips—

"What did you say?" Shawn demanded.

"What?" Sharice asked, disoriented.

"You said something. It sounded like a guy's name."

Fuck. Had she really said Jamal's name out loud? She was really losing it. Quickly, she said, "No, I just moaned. Uh, I probably ought to hang up . . ."

Seconds ticked by.

Finally, he asked, "Wanna come by?"

"No. It's late."

Shawn laughed. "Baby, for what you started, it's still early."

"Well, I've got an early morning today," she lied.

"A'ight. Tomorrow, then?"

A booty call in the offering. Wasn't that what she'd called to set up?

"Let's see how we feel later, okay?"

"Cool. Keep in touch."

He sounded relieved that she didn't want to get together. Or maybe it was happiness she heard?

Sharice shrugged. She didn't care. Whatever it was, she was glad he hadn't pressed the issue. They'd both gotten what they wanted, right? He'd gotten off and she'd gotten . . . gotten . . .

To fantasize about Jamal, about what might have happened if she hadn't left. If she'd had the courage to admit the truth—that she *had* wanted his touch, his desire, his kiss.

All of him.

She started the car, backed out of the parking space, and squealed onto the road. She had somewhere to be.

She only hoped she wasn't too late.

5

Sharice rapped her knuckles against the hotel suite door and waited, listening for the sound of footsteps on the other side.

She heard nothing.

What if Jamal had already gone, left the room despite the fact that he'd paid for the night? She didn't have his phone number. Didn't have his last name. Nor did he have her last name—hell, had she even told him her first name? Anyway, there was no way for them to contact each other.

Sharice chewed her lower lip and raised her hand to knock again. Before her fingers touched the wood, the door opened.

Jamal, shirtless, stood in the doorway.

"Hey," she said, forcing a light smile.

"Hey," said Jamal, unsmiling. His expression neither encouraged nor discouraged.

Sharice kept her eyes on his face, trying not to notice the muscular chest sparsely covered with curly hair, until the eye moved downward to the darker dusting of curlicues peeking above the unbuttoned jeans.

Damn, she wanted him. She wanted to touch him and hold him and press herself against his tight body.

But the indifference that seemed to radiate from him didn't invite that now.

"I didn't think you'd be here," she said.

He raised a brow. "So that's why you came back? Because you didn't think I'd be here?"

"Well, I'd . . . *hoped* you'd be here because . . ." Sharice shrugged, trying to make something serious seem nonchalant. ". . . you were right. "

"Right? About what?"

"Right about the fact that . . ." She shrugged again. "that . . . *that* was what I wanted."

She held her breath, hoping that he wouldn't make her explain what she meant by "that." Prayed that he wouldn't make her say the words she hadn't been able to say earlier.

He stared at her, his eyes dark and unreadable.

She licked her lips. "I want to . . ." *make love* ". . . sleep with you. In the bed."

Her heart thundered against her ribcage.

Her palms felt clammy.

Her face felt warm.

Damn, this is hard.

And still Jamal remained silent.

"Are you going to let me in or do you want me to go?" The indifference in her voice pleased her.

Time seemed to crawl as she and Jamal stood frozen on opposite sides of the door. Finally, he stepped to the side.

Relief whooshed out of her as she entered the room.

After closing the door, Jamal walked through the living room. She followed him, ending up in the bedroom. Stopping at the bed, he unzipped his jeans and slid them down over his lean hips. This time, he wasn't wearing any underwear. His cock was ready to perform.

Damn. Did he stay in a constant state of readiness?

Okay. It looked like they were not going to waste time talking. Which worked for Sharice, since she couldn't believe that she was back here and didn't want to think anymore about what this could mean.

Though her heart jangled in her chest, she smiled. She drew the dress up over her head, then quickly stripped off her bra and panties, making no attempt to make her actions sexy.

Jamal's eyes had changed from brown to black as they slowly traveled down her body and back up. His nostrils flared and a vein throbbed noticeably in his cock, visible from ten feet away.

Obviously, an erotic striptease wasn't a necessary aphrodisiac for him.

Though his gaze never left hers, Jamal reached down and threw the covers back on the bed, then straightened.

Waiting.

Sharice walked forward and climbed into bed, lying on her back. She smiled up at Jamal and stretched sinuously.

She waited.

Jamal slid into bed beside her, then turned her onto her side and pressed his body against her back. She gasped as she felt his hand reach between their bodies and grasp his cock, positioning it, moving it—

Sharice frowned and pressed her butt backward

against him. Where she had previously felt his cock, she felt nothing.

He'd tucked it between his legs.

She turned back to face him. "What are you doing?"

"Giving you what you asked for."

Her frown deepened. "What?"

Jamal's eyes were serious but something seemed off. "You said you wanted to *sleep* with me."

Sharice flopped back onto her back and punched Jamal lightly on the arm.

This time, there was no mistaking his expression. He was smiling.

"You know that I meant—"

She didn't have a chance to finish the sentence, for Jamal leaned forward and captured her mouth with his. His lips moved softly over hers, giving her a kiss meant to stoke passion slowly, to fuel her desire lightly.

He drew back.

Sharice opened her eyes, staring up into eyes that appeared to regard her seriously—for real this time.

"Why'd you come back?" he asked.

Oh, shit. So much for not talking.

She raised her hand to Jamal's chest and trailed her finger between his pecs. "Because after . . ." *phone sex with Shawn* . . . Sharice suppressed a flash of guilt. Not that she had any logical reason to feel guilty. She didn't owe Jamal anything. But she still felt a tad guilty. "Because after I left here, I realized that I didn't want to leave."

"Just like that? All on your own, you came to realize this?"

Another flicker of guilt whizzed through her. Did

he suspect something? No, she was being paranoid. There was no way he could.

"Yes."

He stared intently at her, then looked away, as if something he saw there bothered him. "Earlier, in the bar—"

"Shhhhh," Sharice said, not wanting to talk about anything serious that might ruin her resolve to stay here with him. Moving her hand lower, brushing the hair that had teased her when he'd come to the door, moving even lower, she wrapped her fingers around his cock.

She squeezed.

He gasped.

Sharice raised up and placed her mouth against his, brushing a soft kiss against his lips. "Let's talk later, okay?"

"Alright." Jamal put his hand behind her neck, and pulled her to him. His mouth, once again moving firmly over hers, answered her question. There'd be no talking right now. Not communication that involved logical, rational thought, anyway—which was good because Sharice didn't think she was capable of forming complex sentences—or even simple sentences involving more than two words.

As Jamal's mouth plundered hers and his hands roved her side, she rolled on top of him. Just as she'd imagined being when she'd been on the phone with Shawn.

Only this felt better. Much better. Her hips pressed against his hips, her chest brushed against his chest, teasing her nipples to instant hardness. His hands pulled her body to him, as if he couldn't get close enough. His tongue explored her mouth as if he could not taste enough.

Jamal made her feel as if he could never get enough. Of *all* of her.

Which drove her need higher.

Jamal made her feel cherished.

Which made her heart race.

Jamal made her feel special.

Breaking the kiss, Sharice raised her hips off of him, reached for his cock and placed him between her legs, positioning him right where she wanted him.

While staring into his eyes, Sharice lowered her hips. Jamal glided inside of her, hitting the spot deep within her that made her gasp.

Jamal's eyes turned two shades darker, seeming to lose focus. His lips parted and he moaned, his grip on her ass tightening. "Oh, baby. You feel so good."

"Yeah . . ." was all she could manage. She felt breathless.

Sharice lifted her hips and tore her gaze from his, looking down to where their bodies were connected.

That's what she felt. A connection.

She pumped her hips. Up and down. Slow and then fast.

Once again, Jamal's grip on her hips tightened. This time, to stop her. "Don't move. I can't—"

Sharice stopped long enough to take his hands from her hips and place them by his head, holding them captive.

She shimmied against him.

"Baby." His tone pleaded.

"Jamal." Her tone demanded. "This is what I want."

She squeezed his hands. "Your touch."

She gyrated her hips. "Your desire."

Jamal exhaled heavily.

Sharice leaned down, pressing her mouth against his. "Your kiss. I want all of you."

Jamal groaned. Jerking his hands out from under hers, he placed a hand on the back of her head and pulled her hard against him. His kiss was no longer gentle. It demanded and possessed, his tongue restlessly exploring her mouth, constantly roving as if desperate to discover any secrets that might be hidden there.

Sharice let him explore, meeting his tongue, mating with his mouth, holding nothing back, exposing her secrets—her want, her desire, all for his taking.

His hands moved back to her hips, pushing them up, pulling them down, guiding her faster, urging her deeper.

The familiar heat spread through her body, rushing downward—from her heart to her stomach, upward—from her toes to her thighs, growing hotter.

Jamal's fingers dug into her ass cheeks.

"Now. Please." His voice was pained.

"Now." Her voice was joyous.

"Yes," he said, his body going still while his cock throbbed inside her.

"Yes," she said, her muscles clenching and unclenching around his cock.

They clung to each other, riding the tide of passion together.

As her breathing became regular and her body no longer quaked, Sharice raised her head to look at Jamal. His eyes were closed and a faint smile played on his lips.

She dropped her head back onto his chest.

His hand lightly rubbed her back.

"That was fantastic but . . . please tell me we're done for a bit," she said.

His laughter rumbling against her chest was the last sound she remembered hearing before she fell asleep.

~~~~

Sharice tiptoed to the bedroom door, then turned back for yet another peek. After propping herself on an elbow and watching Jamal sleep for a good fifteen minutes after she'd woken up, she still could not get enough of seeing him.

This time, he was flat on his stomach, his arms thrown out from his sides, the sheet tangled around his legs and covering only his ass.

Sharice licked her lips. If she wasn't running late, she'd go back and slide under the covers, rubbing her hips against his delectable ass, while kissing his neck, his back, before slipping her hands underneath him, searching for his cock—

Her panties felt wet.

Sharice grinned, blew him a kiss, and headed out the door. She'd see him again. She—

Stopped.

Hmmmm.

It didn't feel right to just leave Jamal without a word, like he was just another one-night stand. Something was going on here. Something scary and exciting that she didn't want to put a label on, or think too much about. Something that required her to do more than just skip out on Jamal without a word.

Sharice walked through the dining room to the desk in the corner of the room. Opening the drawer, she removed a piece of hotel stationery, grabbed a pen, and began writing. Finished, she folded the paper and returned to the bedroom.

Jamal was still comatose.

As she reread her note, it dawned on her that this was the first time she'd told Jamal her name. How backward was that? The one guy she cared about hadn't known her name.

Well, he did now.

Smiling, she placed the note on the pillow next to Jamal and kissed his cheek lightly. As she turned to leave, Dr. Love's words flashed through her mind: *Go sin.*

She smiled. Yeah, well, she'd already sinned. Big time.

6

Sharice sat on the barstool, staring at the menu spread open in front of her on the oval table. It felt odd to be at Tantrum in the early evening—she'd always meant to try out the food, but had never been there at dinner time.

Tonight, she had a reason to be there at dinner time. She had a date . . . with Jamal. When was the last time that she'd been out on something as simple, as innocent as a date?

She suppressed a dopey grin—something that she'd found herself having to do ever since she'd left Jamal in the morning. In the midst of preparing her PowerPoint slides for a presentation for an investor meeting, she'd stared blankly at the screen, reliving the feel of Jamal underneath her, thrusting inside of her slowly, then quickly, changing his motion from the usual in-and-out to circular gyrations.

Who would've guessed that the simple, easy motions could've brought her to climax like that?

This time, she couldn't prevent the silly grin from spreading over her face.

"I've never seen anyone that happy about our menu," said a cheery voice.

Busted.

Sharice raised her eyes to the woman standing before her, notepad poised between her red-tipped fingertips. Amusement shone in her eyes.

"Uh. I was thinking of something else."

The woman smiled, obviously deciding that further commentary would constitute prying. "Are you ready to order?"

"No, not yet. I'm waiting for someone."

"Sure. Take your time."

Sharice watched the young woman walk away, a definite swish to her strut. Maybe she'd gotten some this morning, too.

The thought caused Sharice's dopey grin to grow wider.

Smiling was the last thing she thought she'd be doing. The fact that her worst fear had just come true—that she would, indeed, be calling into Dr. Love and reporting her sin, the desire for a r-e-l-a-t-i-o-n-s-h-i-p—should have had her paralyzed by fear. But, instead of feeling afraid, she felt alive, excited. Though she didn't know how long this feeling would last or what the future—if any—held for her and Jamal, she wanted to revel in the feeling. It'd been so long. It'd taken so long to put her heart back together after Malcolm, then Darrell, she'd been unwilling to risk it again.

Until Jamal.

Maybe three was, indeed, the charm. Maybe Jamal would, indeed, prove to be different.

The front door opened. She glanced that way, hoping to see Jamal. It wasn't him but the dark-skinned brotha with the locks looked familiar.

Sharice frowned. Where had she seen him before? At Geoffrey's? At Tantrum? At—

That was it—outside of Tantrum. It was Shawn.

Damn. Maybe he'd turn and walk in the opposite direction.

He turned and walked her way.

Maybe he wouldn't see her.

He looked in her direction and paused by her table. His lips curved into a sexy smile.

Her smile was polite. "Hi, Shawn."

His smile slipped. Confusion skittered across his brow. "Do I know you?"

"Sharice."

"Sharice . . .?"

Sharice frowned. What game was he playing? "We . . . 'spoke' earlier."

"Baby, if you and I spoke, I'd remember."

"Come on. I called you at . . ." Sharice bent down and retrieved her cell phone. She flipped it open and brought up the last call she'd made to Shawn. ". . . at 3:47 A.M. 510-555-9123."

"My number is 510-555-9124."

Sharice's heart raced. Maybe she misheard. "Your number's not 510-555-9123?"

"No . . . Did we meet?"

Sharice stared sightlessly into Shawn's eyes. "I'm sorry . . . I don't mean to be rude but I . . . need to sort this out."

"Hey, maybe I can . . . you know, help you sort things out."

Sharice smiled politely. "No. Thank you."

His smile was sexy. "Sure, babe. Wish it had been me. If you change your mind, call me."

Shawn winked and walked on.

Sharice sat back and closed her eyes.

If she hadn't been talking to Shawn, who the hell had she been calling? Opening her eyes, she jerked upright, opened her cell, and called up the number she thought was Shawn's. As she hit the dial button and the phone began to ring, Jamal slid onto the stool next to her.

"Hey," he said, smiling. He leaned forward and pressed a light kiss against her lips.

"Hey," she said, forcing a smile and debating whether or not to disconnect the call. It wasn't as if she could talk to whomever answered with Jamal right here in front of her.

The phone rang in her ear.

Jamal's phone rang.

She'd just give it one more ring, see if voicemail answered, see if—by some miracle—the greeting had been changed to say his name.

Idly, she glanced over at Jamal.

He was staring at the display of his phone, stunned.

"Is everything okay?" Sharice asked.

Jamal looked up at her, his eyes filled with surprise, shock, and . . . guilt?

"What's wrong?" she asked, deciding the Shawn-who-was-not-Shawn thing could wait.

Jamal's gaze went back to his cell phone.

Sharice disconnected the call.

Jamal's phone died in mid-ring.

While her mind raced at warp speed to put together the puzzle pieces flying through her brain, her eyes seemed to take in Jamal's actions in slow motion.

He flipped his now-silent cell phone closed.

He rubbed the side of the phone with his thumb, not looking at her.

Finally, he returned his gaze to her, his look apologetic.

The puzzle pieces instantly fell into place. "You. It's been you—"

"I can explain."

"Really? Why start now?" She tossed her cell phone into her purse with more force than was necessary. "I can't fucking believe this."

"Sharice, I was going to tell you—"

"When? When were you going to tell me, Jamal?"

"Last night, at the bar. Then, afterwards, in—"

The blood roared past her eardrums, heated her body, and produced a shakiness that made her want to reach out and break something.

Like Jamal's neck.

She spread her hands out in front of her. "So this has all been some sick joke?"

"No!"

"Why? I just want to know why?"

"Look, it's not the way—"

"Oh, forget it." Sharice yanked her purse from the arm of the chair and jumped off of the barstool. "I don't want to know. It doesn't matter."

Jamal reached out a hand, stopping her. "Would you just give me a chance to explain?"

Explain what? How she'd just been made an ass out of?

Again.

How she'd picked the wrong guy to trust?

Again.

What the fuck was wrong with her? Women were credited with intuition that was supposed to guide them to making the right decisions in life. Well, she'd really tried to listen to hers this time. Though, obviously, she must be the only woman born with no intuition.

Or hers was broken.

Sharice jerked her arm out of his grasp.

"Please." The word was issued between gritted teeth.

Oh, geez. As painful as it might be, she really did want to know why, really did want to know what the hell was going on.

"Fine." She plopped back on the stool, crossed her arms, and tapped her fingertips against her forearm.

Jamal looked like he wanted to roll his eyes. He frowned, instead. "Look, let's calm down. I know I should've told you sooner—"

"Sooner?"

This time, he did roll his eyes. "I know I should've told you. But I didn't want to lose you—"

"And that made it okay to lie to me? To pretend to be two people?"

"I only *pretended* to be one person."

"Yeah, well, you pretended to be Shawn and lured me into phone sex with you. Then, as Jamal, had real sex with me." Sharice felt righteous. "Anyway you look at it, you lied."

Jamal's lips tightened. His nostrils flared. "Yeah, well, you lied, too. You had phone sex with Shawn right after having real sex with me." He flung his hands out, like a magician after making a rabbit disappear. "And you didn't tell me. A lie by omission."

Sharice opened her mouth, then closed it.

He had a point. She did lie. When he'd asked her why she'd come back to him, she hadn't mentioned Shawn. Technically, she didn't have to tell him. But in her heart, she'd felt she should've. "You're right. I'm sorry."

But that still didn't excuse him, absolve him of any wrong-doing. That didn't mean he still wasn't wrong for pretending to be Shawn, for leading her on, for—

"I was wrong," Jamal said.

Oh. Okay.

"When I got your first message, I loved your voice. It was sultry, sexy . . ."

Ah, that's nice.

". . . a porn star's voice."

"What?"

"Will you let me finish?"

But, a porn star's voice? Sharice sighed.

"You sounded classy."

A *classy* porn star?

"I'd gotten other calls from women, looking for Shawn, and none of them sounded like you. When I called you back, I was going to tell you not to waste your time with Shawn, that he was a playa . . ." He shrugged. "But then, I heard your voice, and I wanted to meet you. Tell you in person."

"Why didn't you?"

"Because when I met you, I realized you liked playas."

"I don't like playas."

He raised a brow.

"I don't." She didn't. She simply chose them because she understood them; they were comfortable.

They weren't like Jamal.

"Well. I knew you wouldn't go for me. I'm not flashy. I don't do casual sex—usually. But, when you seemed interested in me and since you didn't know I was 'Shawn,' there didn't seem to be a reason to tell you."

"Why didn't you tell me when I called you, after I left the hotel?"

"Because I was angry, that you chose Shawn over me, a casual fuck over what I thought I could give you."

Oh. So she wasn't the only one who felt vulnerable in all this.

Sharice reached for his hand. "I didn't want that. I wanted you but . . . I was afraid of you, of feeling. Shawn was what I was used to, but—" Sharice rubbed her fingers across his skin, momentarily distracted by how good he felt, how good his hands had made her feel as he'd touched her body, strummed her—

"But?"

She turned her attention back to the conversation. "But I wasn't into him. All I could think about was you."

Jamal grinned. "I know. You said my name."

Sharice punched his arm.

He mimicked her voice. "'Oh, Jamal' . . . 'Oh, Jamal.'"

Sharice laughed and socked him again. "Stop it."

"Okay, okay." The laughter faded from his eyes. "Sorry, all right?"

"Yeah," she said softly.

"Let's start again. Hi, I'm Jamal." He stuck out his hand.

Sharice slipped her hand in his. "Hi, I'm Sharice."

"Nice to meet you, Sharice."

He placed a finger under her chin and tipped her head up, seconds before lowering his mouth to hers. Her tongue dipped between his lips, stealing a taste.

A taste of forgiveness and promise and beginnings.

The sound of a throat being cleared caused her to break away. She looked up into the amused expression of a guy with locks. "Got everything sorted out?" he asked.

"Yeah," she said.

"Okay," he winked and clapped Jamal on the back. "You're a lucky brotha," he said and walked away.

Jamal frowned. "Who was that?"

"Shawn."

"Shawn!"

Sharice told him what happened. When she finished, he said, "So that's your type. Pretty boys in designer suits and fancy cars?"

"Jamal, I explained why I went after guys like Shawn. I don't care about material things."

"Really?" He asked, his eyes sparkling.

"Really," she said, frowning.

"Okay, then. Let's go somewhere else to eat. I'll drive."

"Okay," she said, her tone slightly confused. He grabbed her hand and led her out the door and down the street, stopping in front of a red car.

Sharice took one look at the "vintage" Toyota Camry and burst out laughing. Turning to Jamal, she gave him a kiss.

"Yeah, I think you're my type."

AUTHOR'S NOTE

While Sharice and her escapades in *A Sinful Phone Call* are fictional, the Dirty Minnie is not. This drink was created specifically for me by a delightful bartender at Triple Play—a bar located in the Underground in Atlanta, Georgia, while I was doing "research." Here's the recipe:

Dirty Minnie

1½ ounces of Stoli Strasberi
Splash of Stoli Vodka
¾ ounces of Amaretto
Splash of Grenadine
Splash of Sprite
Splash of Sweet and Sour
Garnish with lemon and cherry

It's delicious, but deadly, so drink it with caution. For the story behind the drink, please visit me at www.RachelleChase.com.

ABOUT THE AUTHOR

Rachelle Chase is an award-winning romance author, business consultant, speaker, and model who's appeared on national television—CBS, as well as "The Morning Show with Mike and Juliet"—plus national radio shows, including "Playboy Radio," the "Hip-Hop Connection," and the "Jordan Rich Show."

An excerpt from "Out of Control," a novella in SECRETS VOLUME 13, was used in ON WRITING ROMANCE, published by Writer's Digest Books, to illustrate how to effectively heighten sexual tension in a romance book.

Published works include:

KICKING THE BUCKET LIST (memoir)—
available 2015
A SINFUL FIANCÉ (The Sin Club Book 4)—
available Spring 2015
HOT DREAMS—available Summer 2015
"The Firefighter Wears Prada" in MEN ON FIRE
SEX LOUNGE
A SINFUL STRIPTEASE (The Sin Club Book 1)
A SINFUL PHONE CALL (The Sin Club Book 2)
A SINFUL PROPOSITION (The Sin Club Book 3)
"Out of Control" in SECRETS VOLUME 13

Read more and sign up for her newsletter at
www.RachelleChase.com.

Here's a hot sneak peek at Rachelle Chase's

A Sinful Proposition (The Sin Club Book 3),

available now . . .

1

"*Today* is the day to 'sin,'" Alyssa James said as she plopped down onto the lime green micro-suede chair in her best friend's office. She stared at Shannon, waiting for her response.

"You've got to stop listening to that garbage on the radio," Shannon said absently, not bothering to look up from whatever she was doing on her laptop.

"*The Sin Club* is not garbage. Dr. Love has successful sinners on his show every night. Today is my day."

"You've said that every day for the last 30 days."

"It's the power of positive thinking. I feel that *today* is going to be different."

Shannon shook her head. "How would you even know if you're sinning, Alyssa? You already break all the rules on your online blog."

Shannon had a point. Alyssa had started her blog, Sex in San Francisco, as a joke—she'd grabbed her camera and hit the streets of San Francisco, looking for interesting occurrences to write about. In a park in Pacific Heights, she'd snapped a photo of two dogs— a perfectly coiffed Jack Russell terrier and a scruffy mongrel of unidentifiable heritage—in *flagrante delicto*. Afterward, she'd blogged about how opposites attract, even in the animal kingdom.

How was she to know that Fifi belonged to a prominent politician's wife? And how could she have guessed that the wife would call every radio and television station demanding that Fifi's photo be removed? Alyssa hadn't removed the photo, instead encouraging visitors to participate in the fracas online.

Sex in San Francisco was proof that *all* publicity was good publicity. Alyssa now dished the scoop on the private lives of San Francisco's rich and beautiful. But at a price. Hanging out in bushes and crashing parties left little time for a life of her own. So, while she did, indeed, "sin" for Sex in San Francisco, she had no time for personal sinning.

"I'm talking about sinning in my personal life."

"What personal life?"

"The personal life I'm about to have. I hired an assistant."

"That just means that you'll find more work for both of you to do."

While Alyssa didn't blame Shannon for her skepticism, a little best-friend humoring would've been nice. The negative energy rolling off of Shannon in waves was starting to put a dent in her conviction that today was *the* day.

She sighed. Loudly.

Shannon finally looked up and asked with resignation, "So what personal sin are you finally going to commit today?"

Alyssa grinned. "I'm glad you asked. I'm thinking about sex. After all, shouldn't the blogger of Sex in San Francisco be having sex?"

"Umm-hmm." Shannon's gaze returned to her computer.

"Yeah, I know. I've always been a commitment gal—"

"An understatement," Shannon said. "Three years with Phil, four years with that loser from high school, four years—"

"Well, now I'm thinking, the heck with that. I can't afford the time for a relationship."

"Especially," Shannon muttered, "with the emotionally needy guys you get involved with."

Alyssa ignored that. "But I have time for a fling. If I'm willing to sin. That is, just go up to a hot guy and proposition him."

Shannon snorted. "Now, that I'd like to see. In fact, I'd pay to see that—you propositioning someone."

"Very funny." Alyssa decided to change the subject. "So how's business at The Perfect Date?"

"Slow. You know how tough startups are."

"Yeah."

"If I don't get a burst of business soon, I'm afraid . . ." Shannon sighed. After a minute, she beamed, instantly transformed into the poster child for positive thinking. "But I got a new client today." Once again, she tore her eyes away from her computer screen. "You won't believe who called me to hire a *corporate* escort!"

Alyssa smiled. Shannon always emphasized the word "corporate" lest anyone think she dealt in sexscorts—a term she coined for the less reputable escort services.

"Barney," said Alyssa.

"Barney Gaffney? Why would he need my services?"

"No. I meant Barney, from television. And I can think of one hundred reasons as to why he'd need your services. One, he's dull. Two, he lumbers around—"

Shannon sighed heavily.

Alyssa smiled. "Okay, okay. I'll be serious. Who?"

Before she could answer, the phone rang and Shannon answered. Nanoseconds later, she grinned. "Please send him in, Charlotte."

Shannon stood up.

Alyssa gathered her purse and prepared to stand.

"No. Don't go. I want you to see this."

Alyssa shrugged and settled back into her chair.

The elation in Shannon's face suddenly faded and she directed a stern look at Alyssa. "You *cannot* put this on your gossip blog."

Indignation rumbled in Alyssa's stomach. "I do not deal in gossip. I deal in facts and—"

"Alyssa!"

"Of course I won't. You know I never write about personal or confidential—"

The soft whoosh of the office door opening, coupled with the ass-kissing grin spreading across Shannon's face, stopped Alyssa in mid-protest. Alyssa turned toward the door, desperate to see who could bring such an abomination to the mouth of her no-nonsense friend.

"Mr. Brooks. Please come in," Shannon gushed behind her.

The Mr. Brooks—as in, Tony Alfonso Brooks . . .

as in, owner of Flush, The Gilded Cage, Bubbles, and a dozen other upscale bars . . . as in the very single, very sexy, Antonio Banderas clone whose private life was a mystery.

And here she'd been given a glimpse into that mystery . . . That the most eligible man in The City apparently had to pay to get a date. Priceless. Glee bubbled up inside her. What a great story this would—

Damn. There was no story. She'd just promised Shannon she wouldn't write about him.

How could Shannon do this to me?

Just last week, Alyssa had written a piece speculating on the likelihood that Tony Brooks and supermodel-turned-restaurateur Chantelle Dubois had eloped to Sarlat, France.

Obviously that wasn't true, since he was standing in front of her. So putting Mr. Brooks within touching distance but saying she couldn't write about him was like . . . like . . . putting a fudge sundae in front of a child and saying, "don't eat it."

As Tony glided into the room in a navy Versace suit, Alyssa's racing heart, fluttery stomach, and rise in body temperature told her that he was like a fudge sundae in other ways—delicious, decadent, and deadly.

"Shannon, thanks for seeing me on such short notice." Smiling, he extended his hand to Shannon.

"My pleasure. Before we begin, let me introduce you to Alyssa James."

No, no. Don't introduce me.

". . . Alyssa, this is Mr. Tony Brooks."

Just this once, why hadn't Alyssa listened to her mother? When Alyssa was a teenager, her mom had always stressed to never leave the house without looking one's absolute best. Well, today Alyssa had left the house looking her absolute worst—no makeup, ponytail looped through the back of a "Just Do It" black Nike baseball cap, olive green cargo pants. The only item of clothing saving her from total fashion disaster was her fuchsia Bebe T-shirt.

Tony seemed to agree, for his eyes lingered on her breasts.

Alyssa blushed.

His gaze returned to her face. "She's not quite what I expected but . . . the long brown hair and doe-like eyes definitely work."

Alyssa's mouth dropped open.

Tony's gaze dropped to her mouth. "Nice, pouty lips. A little glossy stuff would help."

Glossy stuff? The nerve, utter gall. Why—

His gaze traveled lower. "Great breasts . . ."

Alyssa's face felt crimson. "How—"

"Kind of hard to make out the rest of her in those unattractive pants, but I'm guessing she's about a size eight?"

Once again, his eyes returned to her face. He raised a brow, as if expecting an answer.

I'm a size six. Alyssa's lips tightened.

His gaze returned to her lips.

Maybe he was imagining them coated in "glossy stuff." Or maybe he was imagining the feel of them against his, pressing and nibbling, while her hand caressed his Michelangelo-carved cheeks, before she trailed her fingers to his black, shoulder-length hair, freeing it from the band that held it, running her fingers—

No. That was her imagination, not his. Silly twit.

Her jaw clenched. "Would you like to see my teeth, Mr. Brooks?"

He seemed to consider the question. "I hadn't thought about it, but it might be a good idea—"

"I am not a horse, Mr. Brooks, and I find your—"

Shannon's laugh had an edge of hysteria. "Don't you just love her sense of humor?"

His eyes narrowed, no longer seeming to assess horseflesh, instead searching for a hint of the sense of humor Shannon had promised.

Alyssa smiled, careful to hide all her teeth.

"Why, just before you arrived we were discussing how *today* was her day."

Alyssa looked at Shannon, whose smile was one step away from a grimace. *Don't fuck this up for me,* her look said.

Don't fuck what up? Alyssa shot back. *I don't know what the hell is going on here. One second I'm talking about* The Sin Club *and the next minute I'm being stripped and—*

Her words echoed in her mind: *Today is the day to "sin."* Shannon was trying to remind her of that.

Alyssa's eyes widened. She jerked her head in Tony's direction. "You want *me* to be his date?"

"You hadn't figured that out?" asked Tony.

"No. I'm not a—"

Tony grinned. "Then you're perfect." He turned back to Shannon. "I'll take her."